# Silverlake Fairy School

## Stardust Surprise

# Silverlake Fairy School

## A magical world
## where fairy dreams come true

Collect the titles in this series:

Unicorn Dreams

Wands and Charms

Ready to Fly

Stardust Surprise

Bugs and Butterflies

Dancing Magic

For more enchanting fairy fun, visit
www.silverlakefairyschool.com

# Silverlake Fairy School
## Stardust Surprise

Elizabeth Lindsay

Illustrated by Anna Currey

USBORNE

For Arthur, apprentice wand maker, with love

First published in 2009 by Usborne Publishing Ltd., Usborne House,
83-85 Saffron Hill, London EC1N 8RT, England.
www.usborne.com

Text copyright © Elizabeth Lindsay, 2009

Illustrations copyright © Usborne Publishing Ltd., 2009

The right of Elizabeth Lindsay to be identified as the author of this work has been
asserted by her in accordance with the Copyright, Designs and Patents Act, 1988.

The name Usborne and the devices 🏆 🎈 are Trade Marks of
Usborne Publishing Ltd.

All rights reserved. No part of this publication may be reproduced, stored
in a retrieval system or transmitted in any form or by any means, electronic,
mechanical, photocopying, recording or otherwise without the prior permission
of the publisher.

This is a work of fiction. The characters, incidents, and dialogues are products
of the author's imagination and are not to be construed as real. Any resemblance to
actual events or persons, living or dead, is entirely coincidental.

A CIP catalogue record for this book is available from the British Library.

UK ISBN 9780746076828   First published in America in 2012 AE.
American ISBN 9780794530655  JFMAMJJ SOND/11 01560/1
Printed in Dongguan, Guangdong, China.

# Contents

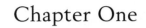

## Chapter One

# Study and Trouble

Three First Year fairies, one purple, one sky-blue and one yellow-ocher, were sitting together in the great library at Silverlake Fairy School. They were poring over a large green and silver leather-bound book. Sunshine streamed in through the high-arched window behind them lighting up the pages perfectly. They were doing their assignment, special after school study, that their teacher, Mistress Pipit, had assigned them. Today she had asked them to find out as much as they could about stardust, in particular, its most important use.

Lila, the purple fairy, was sitting in the middle of the three and keeping her voice low.

"Stardust is collected at the time of the full moon," she read out.

"That's when the moon-wind blows its hardest," whispered Bella, the sky-blue fairy.

"That's what the book says next," said Lila, looking up from the page, surprised.

"Bella, you must have remembered that from last year," said Meggie, the third fairy, brushing her yellow-ocher hair from her eyes. "You have a better memory than you thought."

Of the three Charm One Class fairies, Bella was the only one doing her First Year at Silverlake Fairy School for the second time. She had failed nearly all her exams the previous year.

"One of the nice things about being a First Year twice is when something suddenly pops into your head from last time around," Bella said. "But the nicest thing of all is having you two as my best friends."

"And as your best friends we want you to write down every useful fact we find out about stardust," said Lila, smiling. "Then the information will be at your fingertips ready to be remembered." She quickly made a note about the moon-wind on her own scroll.

"But I know the facts now you've read them out from the book!"

Lila gave Bella a sceptical look.

"You mean you really can remember all of them?" she asked. "I don't believe you."

"Well no, but I can remember some," said Bella. "Oh, I see what you mean, Lila. I suppose I can't remember everything after hearing it only once."

"What else does the book say?" Meggie asked, drawing closer for a better look.

"Loads," said Lila. "Listen to this: 'Stardust

# Stardust Surprise

flows through the sky in glittering showers, hardly ever falling to earth. It cannot be seen during the day, which is why it is collected at night.' And this is interesting, 'Stardust is gathered in wide nets, each net shaped like a dunce's cap. High speed towing is essential to keep the nets inflated'."

"Look at the picture," Meggie said, tapping the page with her finger. "There are eight fairies pulling that net. Eight! No wonder we're not allowed to try it until we're Fifth Years. It looks like it's really hard work."

Lila stared at the picture. "It's more difficult than I thought to catch stardust."

"But definitely lots of fun," Bella said. "The Fifth Years are longing to start practicing. And I can understand why. You get to fly really, really high, at night, in the moonlight and far out of school across the Great Silver Lake. I wish we didn't have to wait so long before we can try it."

"It's something to look forward to," said Lila.

# Study and Trouble

"Anyway, we've got masses to learn before Charm Five, which is why we've got to work hard now and pass our first wand skills exams."

"Okay, okay," said Bella. "I get the point."

"We really want you to stay in our class through the rest of the school," said Lila. "You must pass your exams this time, Bella. You've got to try your hardest."

"I know I do," said Bella. "And I will. I promise."

Lila turned another of the book's pages and then another.

"Ah, this is what we've been looking for. Listen, 'Stardust's most important use is in the making of fairy wands'," said Lila, reading out the answer to Mistress Pipit's question.

"Imagine that," said Meggie, gazing at her own wand. "It's no surprise wands glitter so much considering what they're made from."

"Can we stop now Pipity's assignment is finished for today?" asked Bella, dropping her pencil on the table with a clatter and tapping her scroll with her wand to make it roll up.

"Shush, Bella," whispered Lila, glancing in the direction of Mistress Hawthorn, the librarian. It was true they could stop but Lila didn't want them to get thrown out of the library for being noisy.

"And there's a little more here," she said, reading from a page with the heading 'The Magic of Stardust'. "'It takes many grains of stardust to create one fairy wand and every wand is unique to its owner'."

"What does that mean exactly?" Bella asked.

"It means," said Lila, holding up her own beloved wand, "that I am the only fairy like me and that there is only one wand like mine in the entire Fairy Kingdom. And I love the way my wand matches my purple hair, fingernails and toenails." Lila wiggled her toes under the table. "Your sky-blue wand is the same, Bella. There isn't another one like it. Our wands have been made especially for us." Lila twirled hers until the star at its tip sparkled brightly. She loved learning about its magic.

"If we hadn't come to Silverlake School," said Meggie, "we'd never have been allowed to have our own special wands until we were much older."

"That is so true," said Lila. "Cook didn't get her first wand until she went to cooking school."

Mentioning Cook's name brought memories of working in the Fairy Palace kitchen flooding into Lila's head; of Cook, who had raised her, of her dear friend, Mip, the shoeshine elf and all the other kitchen fairies who were her friends.

"I want to learn as much as I can while I'm here at Silverlake," Lila said. "After all, it was Cook's dearest wish that I came to this wonderful school."

"Me too," said Bella, holding up her wand for attention. "Listen, I've decided I will never fail an exam again. From now on I will work really, really hard."

# Stardust Surprise

"Bella, that's wonderful," said Lila, giving her friend a hug. "Good for you!"

"Only, please, you two, keep helping me. Don't ever let me forget what I've just said."

"We never ever will," said Lila, smiling.

"And we'll always help," promised Meggie.

"I'll work hard at everything, not just the things I love, like flying and playing Bugs and Butterflies matches for the Star Clan," said Bella, her eyes shining. "I will pass all my charm exams or go pop, you see if I don't."

"You've got to pass," giggled Lila. "It would be awful to see you go pop."

Bella grinned at her.

Meggie's attention was back on the great book and she couldn't resist turning over to the next page. She let out an excited gasp.

"Look at this diagram." All three fairies peered eagerly at the picture. "It shows how a stardust net is made."

# Study and Trouble

"Let's copy it," said Lila.

Passing their table a few minutes later, Mistress Hawthorn nodded in satisfaction at the three hard-working fairies.

Eventually, Meggie looked up. "I've finished," she whispered.

"Me too," said Lila, putting down her rainbow pencil.

"Hang on," said Bella. "I can't draw as fast as you two."

The patter of dainty feet crossing the ancient oak floor distracted them. An elegant pink fairy in a flowing gossamer dress and a sea-blue fairy carrying two scrolls, were coming toward them.

"Here's trouble," said Lila, quickly rolling up her work. "Hurry up, Bella. It's Princess Bee Balm and Sea Holly."

"I haven't finished," said Bella.

"It's okay," said Meggie. "You can copy mine."

"That's not the point," said Bella, continuing to

draw. "We can't be running off every time Bee Balm and Sea Holly arrive."

"Bella's right," said Lila, after a pause. "We have as much right to be here as Bee Balm does. And if she doesn't like it, well, rosehips to her."

The Princess stopped and ran her eye along the shelf beside them until she came to the empty space left by the green and silver book. She turned with a frown to the three friends.

"You've got *Stardust and Its Uses.* I want it," the Princess said.

Meggie stood up and smiled politely. "We've almost finished with it."

"I don't care whether you've finished or not. Hand it over."

Bella continued writing.

"You heard what Meggie said," Lila added, standing up as well. "We've almost finished. When we have, it'll be your turn. Okay?"

The Princess stamped her foot but Bella refused

to look up. Bee Balm and Sea Holly moved closer and, for one dreadful moment, Lila thought that they were going to snatch the book. But worse, the Princess pointed her wand threateningly.

"I suppose you've forgotten fairies are not supposed to use their wands in anger against other fairies," said Bella.

"Well, well," said Bee Balm. She gave Bella a considered look. "You're not as empty-headed as you pretend. You *can* actually remember school rules." Bella glared, Bee Balm flicked her wrist and the book slammed shut on top of Bella's hand. The noise echoed around the library.

"Bee Balm!" All five fairies turned to see Mistress Hawthorn advancing toward them. "How dare you come into the library and create a disturbance."

"I was only asking when *Stardust and Its Uses* might be free," said Bee Balm, looking her most innocent.

# Study and Trouble

"Blundering boggarts," said Bella under her breath, pulling her hand from between the pages and rubbing her bruised fingers.

"Serves you right," Bee Balm hissed at Bella. "Next time I want something you just give it to me. Okay?"

"Harebell, Bee Balm, pay attention and listen to me. I will not have precious library books slammed shut in that disgraceful way," the librarian said.

"It wasn't me!" said Bee Balm.

"Which one of you was it then?" asked Mistress Hawthorn looking in turn from one fairy to another. Lila had seen Bee Balm use her wand but the Princess said nothing. "I see, no one will own up. Very well, Lilac Blossom, Harebell and Nutmeg, lose a Star Clan point each." Lila caught the smug look on the Princess's face. "Bee Balm and Sea Holly, you two caused the disturbance, lose two Sun Clan points." There was a pause while Bee Balm drew breath. "Each," added Mistress Hawthorn.

"That's not fair," Bee Balm exploded. "We didn't do anything."

"I can add a detention to that if there's any answering back, Bee Balm. Lilac Blossom and Nutmeg, put the book back on the shelf." Lila and Meggie hurried to do as they were told. "And now each one of you will leave my library and not return to it until you can be trusted to treat these valuable books with respect."

Bee Balm swished her pink gossamer frock and marched proudly to the door, with Sea Holly scurrying after her. Lila, Meggie and Bella trailed out behind them.

"Who does Bee Balm think she is?" muttered Bella, as Mistress Hawthorn watched them go with a gritty stare.

Lila was equally furious, knowing the Princess had disliked her intensely from the moment she

# Study and Trouble

realized they both wanted to go to Silverlake Fairy School. Bee Balm constantly made it clear that she hated being at school with a fairy from the palace kitchen and insisted on being Lila's sworn enemy. It made life very difficult.

Once they were safely in the Hall of Rainbows Bee Balm pounced on the three friends.

"I suppose you think getting me thrown out of the library was really smart, Miss Pots-and-Pans," she snapped. "Now how am I supposed to finish my assignment?"

"And me!" Sea Holly joined in.

"Give me yours," the Princess said, snatching at Lila's scroll. But Lila quickly swung it out of reach.

"Don't you dare let her have it, Lila," said Bella. "You started the trouble by slamming the book, Bee Balm. And you lied about it. We've all lost clan points because of you. If you can't do your assignment that's your problem."

# Stardust Surprise

"Whatever work I do it will be better than yours," snapped the Princess. "Miss Class Mud-Brain."

"Don't you dare call me a mud-brain," said Bella, with eyes blazing. "I'm smarter than you. You wait and see. Just because you're a princess doesn't make you best at everything."

"It makes me better than you, Harebell." And without a backward glance, Bee Balm fluttered up the Owl staircase with Sea Holly following as fast as she could.

"That's it, run for safety when you're losing an argument," Bella shouted after her. Lila took her friend's arm.

"There's no point in getting angry," she said.

"But I am," wailed Bella. "They made us lose clan points. And that's not going to make us popular with Musk Mallow. She hates it when that happens. And rightfully so. She's a really good Head of Clan fairy. Of course she's going to mind and so do I."

# Study and Trouble

Members of all four of the Silverlake Fairy School clans, Star, Sun, Moon and Cloud, were trying to win the most clan points so their clan would come out on top at the end of the school year.

"Well," said Lila, "we'll just have to explain to Musk Mallow exactly what happened. And as Bee Balm and Sea Holly didn't get their assignment done, they're going to look pretty silly in lessons tomorrow if they can't answer any of Pipity's questions."

"But Bee Balm'll just copy the assignment from somebody else," scowled Bella. "Some silly fairy will break another school rule to please her."

"At least she didn't get your scroll," said Meggie to Lila.

"I had no intention of giving it to her." But even so Lila felt miserable. "Everything was going so nicely and now we've had another squabble." Lila sighed. She did try hard to avoid quarrels with the Princess but somehow they just kept happening.

## Chapter Two

# Confessions

Lila, Bella and Meggie hurried from the Hall of Rainbows and quickly fluttered up the Owl staircase to the Star Clan turret. They scurried through the common room, avoiding the other chattering Star Clan fairies, to the bedroom they shared together.

"Let's keep what happened in the library to ourselves," Lila said, closing their door. "We don't want everyone getting cross and making things worse. I hate it when Bee Balm gets my friends into trouble as well as me." Lila dropped her scroll on the table.

"We'll tell Musk Mallow when it's lights out," agreed Meggie.

"Good idea," said Bella.

Lila was not going to let Bee Balm ruin the rest of the evening. She'd secretly been practicing a new charm and decided now was the time to try it on her friends to cheer them all up. She swung around and pointed her wand at Bella with a grin. "Surprise!" she cried.

Bella found herself rising gently toward the ceiling and turned onto her back laughing.

"How did you do that?" she cried. "Look, I'm not using my wings."

"What does it feel like?" Lila asked, keeping her wand steady.

"It's fantastic! If the wind blew I'd disappear through the window and float away like a feather."

"I've practiced with the waste-paper basket, my

scroll and even a chair. Hold tight," Lila laughed.

Bella floated around the room as if lying on a comfy cushion before dropping gently onto her bed.

"Fantastic, Lila," laughed Bella leaping to the floor. "You try, Meggie."

"All right," said Meggie. "It looks fun."

Lila pointed her wand carefully and Meggie drifted into the air and across the room.

"It's strange to float without using my wings," she cried. "But it's lovely and relaxing."

"Lila, teach me and Meggie to do it," said Bella.

"Okay," said Lila. "It's only slightly more complicated than a basic levitation charm," and she demonstrated the wand movements. The charm involved careful pointing and a steady wrist. It wasn't long before Meggie had managed to make Lila float from one side of the ceiling to the other.

"That's enough for me now," said Meggie. "I want to finish the little bag I'm making for Weaving Club."

"I'm not stopping," said Bella. "It's the get-Lila-around-the-room challenge."

Meggie went to the closet and retrieved her little bag. Sewing and weaving were the things she loved doing more than anything else and learning how to do it correctly in a school club gave her great satisfaction.

"How's it coming along?" Lila asked, waiting for Bella's charm to lift her from the floor.

"It's nearly finished. We're going to put in the drawstrings at the next meeting. And I'm going to sew on my yellow mark now so everyone knows it's mine."

Lila suddenly found herself floating. It was a lovely feeling but when Bella lost concentration she dropped, equally suddenly, to the ground again.

# Confessions

"Not bad but you need a little more practice," she laughed.

"At least I got you floating," said Bella, pleased with her success.

There was a knock on the door and Musk Mallow came in smiling. That meant she couldn't have found out about the lost clan points. Lila, Bella and Meggie hurriedly stood in a line.

"We're very sorry, Musk Mallow," said Lila. "We lost three Star Clan points in the library."

Musk Mallow's smile disappeared. "Three points!" she exclaimed. "What happened?"

"It wasn't our fault," said Bella.

"We were doing our assignment and getting the answers from *Stardust and Its Uses* but it was the book Bee Balm wanted and we hadn't quite finished with it, so she used a charm to slam it shut on Bella's hand," Meggie explained.

"And she wouldn't own up to doing it," said Bella.

# Stardust Surprise

"We couldn't say anything," added Lila. "It would have been tattling."

"Oh dear, oh dear, oh dear," said Musk Mallow, shaking her head. "What a lot of trouble Bee Balm can cause."

"We'll earn lots more clan points to make up," said Lila. "We'll work hard to do it."

"Yes, we will, really we will," added Bella.

"I expect nothing less," said Musk Mallow. "Just keep away from Bee Balm as much as possible. Go on, get ready for bed now. Lights out in five minutes. And tomorrow, please, stay out of trouble."


The next morning Lila woke with a start thinking she was at home. But she was snug in her little bed in the Star Clan turret bedroom with Meggie asleep on one side of her and Bella on the other. She shook her wrist and her school bracelet slid up her arm.

# Confessions

"Hello, little unicorn," she whispered to the silver charm that hung from it.

The unicorn was Lila's first Silverlake Fairy School charm. Every fairy pupil received one as a special gift on their first day at school along with their wand. Meggie's charm was a pair of tiny scissors and Bella's, an elfin hat. Lila felt lucky to have been chosen by a unicorn. She believed that, if she could bring it to life, it would take her galloping through the sky on its back. Fairy Godmother Wimbrel, their Headteacher, had once told her to find out the unicorn's name, but even though Lila had tried many guesses, it was still a mystery.

She tried again, giving the charm a gentle tap with her wand. "Galloper," she whispered. "Prancer! Dancer! Racer! Pacer!" But nothing happened.

The early morning bells rang and Lila jumped from her bed. Bella peeked out from under the sheets looking tousled and sleepy.

"It can't be time to get up already," she grumbled.

Laughing, Lila and Meggie pulled Bella out of bed. They soon joined the other fairies hurrying from the Star Clan turret to have their breakfasts.

"Best meal of the day," said Bella, perking up at the smell of heather honey porridge as they came into the refectory. "I'll have two bowlfuls at least." They sat down and between mouthfuls of porridge, ran their eyes down their scrolls. Bee Balm, Sea Holly and the Princess's other admirers were on the opposite side of the First-Year table and Lila kept a watchful eye on them. The Princess was paying particular attention to Candytuft, a Cloud Clan fairy, who was desperate to become her favorite.

"I do believe they've persuaded Candytuft to let them copy her assignment," said Lila, nodding her head in Bee Balm's direction.

# Confessions

"Are we surprised?" Bella said, rolling her eyes. "No, we are not."

"Poor Candytuft," sighed Meggie. "She'll do anything for the teeniest bit of attention from the Princess even though Bee Balm's always so unkind to her."

"Nothing good will come of it," agreed Lila, feeling both sorry for Candytuft and cross with her for being so silly.

Bella tapped her scroll. "Let's review what we found out about stardust. I'm going to prove to Bee Balm that I am not the mud-brain she thinks I am."

Lila quickly put her hand over Bella's work and asked, "Why do fairies collect stardust?"

Bella put both hands to her head. "Because it's infused with magical properties?" she said in a rush.

"Why does stardust almost never fall to the ground?" asked Meggie.

# Stardust Surprise

"Oh, acorns! Yes, yes, I know this, because the moon-wind keeps blowing it through the sky."

"And what is its most important use?" Lila asked.

Bella lowered her voice. "Its most important use is in the making of fairy wands."

"And why do we have to be careful how we use our wands?" Meggie added. "And be exact when we make a charm."

"I don't know," said Bella.

"Think," said Lila.

"So we don't ever harm another fairy when doing magic?" Bella said.

"Correct," said Meggie.

Bella looked down the table thoughtfully. "Do you think Bee Balm meant to slam shut *Stardust and Its Uses*?"

"I'm sure she did," said Lila.

"You see, I don't think she'd care if she harmed another fairy when doing magic, just so long as she got what she wanted," Bella continued.

# Confessions

"The trouble is, back at the Fairy Palace, the Lord Chamberlain spoils her," said Lila. "Bee Balm always gets her way. And I think it's possible the Lord Chamberlain's secretly taught her extra charms to give her an advantage at school. For a start, how did she know the slamming charm?"

"You could be right, Lila," said Bella. "We've never done 'book slamming' in class."

"Of course we haven't, or any kind of slamming," said Meggie.

"It makes me want to be a million times better than she is," said Bella, with determination.

## Chapter Three

# Magical Moments

When the lesson bells rang, Lila, Meggie and Bella hurried to join the rest of the First Years outside their classroom door. Bee Balm and Sea Holly walked to the front of the line as if it was theirs by right and nobody argued with them. The three friends stayed out of the way at the back. Candytuft bobbed up and down behind Bee Balm hoping she would get noticed again, as she had been in the refectory, but the Princess ignored her.

# Magical Moments

A trill of fairy bells rang out and the special orange glowtone that lit up the corridor flickered as Mistress Pipit arrived fluttering her sparkling wings. With a wave of her orange wand the classroom door opened and her pupils filed inside.

"Good morning, fairies," said the teacher.

"Good morning, Mistress Pipit," chanted the class.

When everyone was seated at their mushroom desks and had laid down their wands and scrolls, Mistress Pipit surveyed their eager faces. "We're going to have an exciting morning," she told them. "But first, I'd like to hear what you've found out about stardust."

Hands shot up all around the room, including Bella's. Mistress Pipit noticed it right away.

"Harebell," she said, giving Bella a rare chance to go first.

"We found out that stardust's most important

use is in the making of wands. It's what makes them magic. Stardust has magical properties."

"Well, done, Bella," said Mistress Pipit, with a pleased smile.

"Stardust has magical properties" and "the most important use for stardust is in the making of wands" appeared magically on the board.

"The obvious answer," a voice muttered from the front.

"I'm glad you think so, Bee Balm," said Mistress Pipit. "That was the question I set for your assignment. I didn't notice your hand go up. What else did you find out?"

"What else?" echoed Bee Balm, scrabbling to open her scroll.

"No, don't look," said Mistress Pipit. "Just tell me something that you remember."

Bee Balm looked blank. "I can't think of anything."

"I'll collect a few more facts from the rest of

the class, Bee Balm and come back to you," said Mistress Pipit. "Candytuft."

"I found out that in the Fifth Year we'll collect stardust," said Candytuft, from near the front.

"Excellent, as indeed you will," said Mistress Pipit and Candytuft's answer added itself to the board. "Nutmeg?"

"Stardust is kept in bags woven from spider thread, the strongest thread in the Fairy Kingdom."

"Well done, Meggie."

Bee Balm made a face but Mistress Pipit didn't notice. She had already turned to Periwinkle, another Star Clan fairy.

"Stardust is stored in a secret vault underneath the Fairy Palace," Periwinkle said.

"Yes, but not quite all of it," said Mistress Pipit. "Lilac Blossom?"

"Some is collected and kept here at Silverlake Fairy School," said Lila.

"Yes," said Mistress Pipit.

# Stardust Surprise

While three more facts were added to the list on the board, Lila imagined herself on the back of a handsome unicorn galloping across a moonlit sky pulling a net and collecting stardust. *One day*, she told herself. *One day, it might really happen.*

Lila came back to earth with a start when Mistress Pipit said, "And now Bee Balm, you've had plenty of time to think, is there anything you would like to add to our list?"

"There's so much stuff on the board there's nothing I can think of," said the Princess.

"What a pity," said Mistress Pipit, turning to the others.

"If you can keep all those facts in your head I will have a really knowledgeable class. Now listen carefully. Your Wand Skills Charm Examination will take place in one week's time," she announced to a gasp from her pupils. "There will be a written paper and a practical test. The practical test will be done together as a class. Make sure you learn all the stardust facts we've talked about today for the written paper. I hope you can manage that, Bee Balm?"

"Of course I will," said the Princess. "I have never failed an exam in my life."

"Oh, help," whispered Bella. "This is suddenly really scary."

"There's nothing on the board we don't have written on our scrolls," whispered back Lila. "You'll pass the written test easily. And we can always do some more reading in the library."

"If we're ever allowed back in," Bella groaned.

Mistress Pipit clapped her hands for everyone's attention. "Now, we are going to try a little experiment," she announced.

Mistress Pipit opened up her special storage cabinet next to the board and took something out.

"It's a little bag like the one you're making in Weaving Club, Meggie," said Lila.

# Stardust Surprise

"That's right," said Mistress Pipit. "Would you like to tell the class about it, Nutmeg?"

"Well, it's called a web-woven bag. The yarn is made from spider's thread. And stardust can be stored safely in these little bags because not a single grain can escape."

"Yes, that's quite right, all web-woven bags must be perfectly made for that reason."

Mistress Pipit opened the bag and placed a single grain of stardust on the orange sun at the tip of her wand. "Keep well back," she ordered. "My wand will create a reaction with the stardust now!" The words were no sooner out of her mouth than the stardust exploded into a stream of tiny silver stars and golden suns that flew at high speed around the classroom like mini comets. The fairies gasped and shaded their eyes as the stars whizzed past them, narrowly missing ears, eyes and noses.

"Now you can see for yourselves how powerful one tiny grain of stardust is when it comes into contact with a fairy wand," said Mistress Pipit, as the comets slowed and ended up dancing near the ceiling like tiny fireflies. It had been a spectacular demonstration. "It's always difficult to judge how unpredictable a single grain might be, but by showing you, I hope I've made you cautious."

"I'd never dare do that," said Meggie.

"Quite right, Nutmeg," said Mistress Pipit. "You must only use stardust with the supervision of a teacher. Please remember that. Now we have lots of little lights bouncing around near the ceiling, all the result of the stardust magic. As an experiment I want each of you to catch a light with the tip of your wand. It's not dangerous but hang on to your wands and be prepared for some surprising reactions."

Bee Balm's eyes were alight and she joined in this group activity with more enthusiasm than Lila had ever seen before, swishing her wand wildly.

# Magical Moments

The classroom was soon a riot of fluttering fairies. It was great fun. The light Lila caught made her spin around and around, faster and faster, until the classroom became a blur. By the time it had used up all its energy Lila was thoroughly giddy. She landed breathless just in time to see the light on Bella's wand burning like a white flame before fading.

"Is your wand singed?" she asked.

"No," said Bella. "The flame was fantastically bright, wasn't it?" Meggie's wand whizzed to the ceiling streaming stars behind it. Meggie whizzed after it.

"I let go by mistake," she called down when she finally caught it again.

Lila noticed one last little light near the ceiling, and flew up to catch it. She didn't see that Bee Balm was also chasing it until the Princess shoved her roughly out of the way, knocking her arm so hard that Lila dropped her wand.

# Stardust Surprise

"You hit me on purpose," said Lila, rubbing her elbow and glaring.

"Prove it, Purple Toes! Kitchen Skivvy."

"Bee Balm!" said Mistress Pipit, silencing the whole class. "Not another word. How dare you both disrupt the lesson like that? I'll talk to you two later." She turned to the rest of the class. "Sit down, everyone, please."

"Here's your wand, Lila," whispered Bella, who with a lucky leap had managed to catch it.

Lila was fed up. It was only thanks to Bella her wand wasn't broken. And after such a public argument Lila knew there was trouble to come. Mistress Pipit hated disturbances in her lessons.

When everyone was quiet the teacher continued.

"Now I've demonstrated to you how magical and explosive stardust can be in the open air when it's set off using the tip of a wand. But when it's actually part of a wand the magic works differently. Yes, Bee Balm?"

# Magical Moments

"Would it be possible to make a wand more magical by adding stardust to it so it could make more powerful charms?" Bee Balm asked. "Not like just now when the stardust just exploded."

"Yes, it's possible," replied Mistress Pipit. "But it's not recommended. Remember, everyone, your wand is your most valuable possession. Always take great care of it." Lila held hers more tightly. She certainly intended to do so after dropping it in the lesson.

The bells rang for lunchtime and Mistress Pipit put her little web-woven bag of stardust back in the cabinet. She waited for everyone's attention.

"This afternoon, we'll be doing a practical wand skills lesson by the Bewitching Pool. Meet me there. Bee Balm and Lilac Blossom wait behind, please. The rest of you may go."

Lila glanced miserably at Bella and Meggie. She hoped she wasn't going to lose more Star Clan points. But Bee Balm didn't seem to mind being kept behind. She kept glancing at Mistress Pipit's cabinet as though she was trying to figure something out. Lila hugged her wand and stared at her toes thinking how impossible it was to understand Bee Balm and worrying that, because of the Princess, she was going to get into trouble again.

## Chapter Four

# The Power of Wands

After escaping from the classroom Lila went down to the Hall of Rainbows. Bella and Meggie rushed up to find out what had happened.

"She's given us lines for arguing in class," said Lila. "We've got to do them in the library this afternoon after lessons."

"Whooping wellipedes, that means you'll be sitting right under old Thorny's nose," said Bella.

Lila tried to smile in order to cover up how

upset she was but couldn't manage it. She hated being in Mistress Pipit's bad books. Meggie gave her arm a sympathetic squeeze and Lila had to blink back tears.

"Come on," said Bella, seizing Lila's other arm. "Forget about all that. It's lunchtime and I'm starving."

By the time the silver bells rang for the end of lunch break Lila was feeling a little better. After all, as Bella kept reminding her, she hadn't lost any more clan points. Hurrying, the three friends joined the rest of Charm One Class by the Bewitching Pool ready for the wand skills lesson, just ahead of Mistress Pipit, who arrived carrying an orange gossamer bag. Bee Balm was looking extremely cheerful, Lila noticed, for a fairy who had hundreds of lines to write at the end of lessons. She pushed this bleak thought from her mind as the class gathered around their teacher, waiting to hear what they were going to do.

"This afternoon, we're going to work on transformation charms in preparation for the practical section of the Wand Skills Examination," announced Mistress Pipit. "Divide into teams of three, please."

Lila, Bella and Meggie chose each other and Lila was surprised to see that Bee Balm and Sea Holly had asked Candytuft to join them. The little green fairy was looking unhappy about this arrangement, which was odd considering she was always trying to be included in the royal group.

"Now teams, form a circle around me," instructed Mistress Pipit. Bella was grinning from ear to ear which made Lila expect an exciting lesson. Everyone had eyes on Mistress Pipit's orange bag and watched with interest as she emptied six crumpled-up balls of white paper onto the grass. She circled, then pointed her wand. "Paper worms," she said in a clear and commanding voice. There was a puff of orange suns from her wand and each of the six paper balls changed shape and began to move like worms. Mistress Pipit quickly gathered them up and gave one to each team.

"They're perfectly harmless," she said, putting one in Lila's hand.

Lila inspected it closely. It was the strangest thing she had ever seen. Definitely made of paper, white, with two black eyes and a concertina-like body, it wiggled between her fingers.

"I don't think I like it," Meggie said. "It rustles."

"It's made from paper, Meggie. Paper rustles," said Bella.

"I think it's cute," said Lila. "If I put it on the ground will it still wiggle?"

"You might lose it," Bella warned.

"Paper worms are perfect for practicing transformation charms," Mistress Pipit told them.

# The Power of Wands

"Keep focused and be exact with your wands. But if the charm goes wrong no harm will be done. Lilac Blossom, may I borrow your worm?" Lila handed it to Mistress Pipit. "Pay careful attention everyone. The charm works like this; circle with your wand, and, keeping the arm straight, give an accurate point, followed by a voice command." She dropped the paper worm in order to show them and, with a quick circle and point of her wand she said, "Grasshopper!" in a loud, clear voice. There was a puff of tiny suns and the worm was transformed.

The class gave appreciative cries and the grasshopper jumped. Mistress Pipit quickly took aim and said, "Butterfly." Puff, and a butterfly fluttered skyward. Circle, point, and "Feather!" Puff, a small feather fluttered to the grass. "Paper worm!" And there was the worm again. The fairies applauded and their teacher smiled. Mistress Pipit gave the paper worm back to Lila.

# Stardust Surprise

"I want to see your transformations as swift as that by the end of the lesson. Take turns in your teams. Help each other out if something goes wrong and don't try anything too complicated. Call me if you need help."

The fairies spread out across the grass.

"Meggie, why don't you go first?" said Bella.

Meggie positioned her wand, gave a little nod and Lila put the worm on the ground. It wiggled off immediately. Meggie circled and pointed her wand.

"Elf hat!" she commanded. There was a puff of silver stars and a burst of giggles from Bella.

One half of the paper worm had been transformed into part of a green hat. The rest of the worm was still wiggling underneath it. It did look funny, and Lila wanted to laugh too, but Meggie looked upset so she didn't. "Try again," she said instead.

"Elf hat!" Meggie commanded. This time her aim

was better and a little green elf hat sat on the grass.

"Me next," cried Bella, circling and pointing her wand. "Black bat!" But Bella was in far too much of a hurry. It wasn't a bat that flew into the air but an elf hat with bat's wings.

"My turn," cried Lila, fluttering after the strange flying hat as it made its way clumsily toward the Wishing Wood. When she was close enough, she circled and pointed her wand, crying out, "Walnut," which was the first thing that came into her head. She peered through the puff of purple stars. "Where did it go?"

"It fell through that tree over there," said Bella, catching up.

Lila and Bella fluttered down between the branches.

"Wait for me," called Meggie, joining them.

The three fairies searched the ground.

"Found it," said Lila, picking up a little brown nut.

Suddenly Bella grabbed Lila's arm and put a

# Stardust Surprise

finger to her lips. Meggie was listening too. Voices were coming toward them and one of them sounded like Bee Balm's. The three fairies fluttered silently up into the branches of the nearest tree. None of them wanted another confrontation.

"Did you get it, Candytuft?" snapped Bee Balm.

"Yes," nodded Candytuft.

"Hand it over then."

"But...I feel..."

"No buts about it," said the Princess cutting her off. "You said you'd do anything I asked. Now give it to me."

It was obvious that whatever Candytuft had found for the Princess she was now feeling uncomfortable about it. Something changed hands.

"Good. Now whose turn is it?" asked Bee Balm, putting whatever it was in her pocket. "We want our team to be best at this transforming, hard though it is with a puny school wand."

"It's my turn," said Sea Holly.

"It's mine actually," said Candytuft. "I've only had one turn."

"You can go again after me and Sea Holly," said Bee Balm and the three fairies disappeared back toward the garden.

"Did anyone see what it was that Candytuft handed over?" Bella asked. Lila shook her head, but she had an awful feeling that Bee Balm was up to something.

"Poor Candytuft," said Meggie. "She wants to be the Princess's friend. But why when Bee Balm's so nasty to her?"

"Let's face it," said Lila. "If Bee Balm was a nicer fairy we'd all want to be friends with her. Knowing a princess is kind of special." Lila tossed the walnut into the air. "Your turn, Meggie."

As it came down to land, Meggie said, "Red rose bush."

"Wow, that was clever," said Lila. "What a lovely color."

# The Power of Wands

"But not for long," cried Bella, flicking and pointing her wand. "Paper dart!" The dart was really fast and swooped down toward the Bewitching Pool. The three fairies chased after it and Lila took aim with her wand crying, "Frog!"

Lila's aim was perfect but unfortunately Bee Balm chose that precise moment to flutter in front of the dart. The Princess disappeared in a puff of stars and a glint of bracelet while the paper dart continued on its way. A pink and green frog landed on the grass and with one great hop it jumped into the Bewitching Pool and was gone.

"Oh, no," said Lila, a look of horror on her face. "What have I done?"

The paper dart came skimming back over the pond's surface. "Paper worm," said Bella, catching it as it fell. "Come on, Lila. We must tell Pipity it was a mistake right away or we'll never hear the end of it."

## Chapter Five

# Frog Shock

As soon as they told her what had happened Mistress Pipit hurried to the Bewitching Pool. The rest of the class gathered around to look. The glistening surface of the water stretched before them, broken by pattering droplets from the mermaid fountain. Lila peered into the depths. Fish and frogs swam between the stems of the water lilies but which one was Bee Balm?

"There," said Bella. "Can you see it, Mistress Pipit? The green frog with the pink stripes down its back. That must be Bee Balm."

"Oh, yes," said the teacher, pointing her wand. "Don't worry, Lilac Blossom. She'll be back to normal in a trice."

When the furious Princess emerged from the water Mistress Pipit held out her hand and pulled her, squelching, up the bank.

"I'm soaked," Bee Balm spluttered. "Look at the state of me."

"It was an accident, my dear," soothed Mistress Pipit. "There's no harm done."

"Yes, there is. My frock'll never be the same again." She turned on Lila. "It was you, trying to get back at me, wasn't it?"

"No," said Lila. "It was a genuine mistake. I was aiming at the paper dart."

With a tap of her wand Mistress Pipit dried Bee Balm's dress.

"Bee Balm, I would have thought it was rather interesting being a frog for five minutes," the teacher said. "There's certainly no need for such a fuss. Accidents do happen and I'm here to put them right." Mistress Pipit was firm.

Bee Balm's eyes narrowed dangerously but she said nothing else. Snatching up her wand from the grass she joined Sea Holly and the wide-eyed Candytuft.

"The lesson is going well, considering," said Mistress Pipit. "Only please do take care not to transform each other if you can possibly avoid it. Although I must say Lilac Blossom, your wand skills are coming along. Transforming a princess into a frog is not an easy task." Mistress Pipit's eyes twinkled, and for a second Lila felt pleased, until she caught sight of Bee Balm's furious glare.

The lesson continued until the bells sounded, by which time Lila had made a hare, a dove, and best of all a miniature unicorn. She couldn't help noticing that Bee Balm had not had a successful lesson. She had tried to make a real cat but had only managed a stuffed toy and her golden throne was so wobbly that it fell over. She was in a very bad mood and practically stomped on her wand with frustration.

"You're great at transformation, Lila," Bella told her.

"I have a really good wand," said Lila.

"Don't be nuts," said Bella shaking her head. "It's not just the wand, it's you."

"Quiet, everyone," said Mistress Pipit. "Turn all transformations back into paper and put the pieces into my bag." While everyone was doing this she turned to Bee Balm and Lilac Blossom. "You two go straight to the library. Mistress Hawthorn's expecting you. The rest of the class is dismissed until tomorrow." There was a great wail from the Princess. "What is it now, Bee Balm?" asked their exasperated teacher.

"My school bracelet! It's gone."

"Wait!" said Mistress Pipit. "Wait, everyone.

# Stardust Surprise

Please help Bee Balm search for her bracelet."

The class began to scour the grass. Lila, Bella and Meggie crawled on their hands and knees for ages in case they missed it.

"It must be in the pool," said Bella.

"You're right," said Lila. "I saw it glint as Bee Balm transformed into a frog. It must be in the water."

Mistress Pipit stood by the Bewitching Pool and raised her wand, sending a shower of tiny suns bouncing across the water and diving beneath the surface. Lila's spirits lifted when she thought that her teacher would find the bracelet, but the bouncing suns returned without it. Mistress Pipit clapped her hands.

"I'm not sure where your bracelet's gone," she told the anxious Princess. "I've searched the pond as best I can. Keep searching, Bee Balm and remember, don't leave the castle grounds. I'm sure I don't need to remind you that you won't get back in without

the bracelet and, for that matter, neither will the door of the Hall of Rainbows open for you. I suggest a friend stays with you at all times to help you in and out. This really is unfortunate. I don't think it's ever happened before."

Lila was not in the mood to feel sorry for Bee Balm although if she had lost her own bracelet and silver unicorn she would have been devastated. And it would be unthinkable to be locked out of school. She was convinced that the bracelet was in the Bewitching Pool but there was nothing she could do about it. It was time to write the dreaded lines.

Flouncing ahead with her friends, Bee Balm looked over her shoulder, as if daring Lila to get too close. The Princess's admirers opened the door to the Hall of Rainbows and waited while she walked graciously through it. The Princess was supposed to be treated like an ordinary fairy but Candytuft even dropped a curtsy. Bella scowled and rolled her eyes, which made Lila laugh.

With a wry smile, Lila said goodbye to Meggie and Bella in the Hall of Rainbows.

"Don't try any transformation charms on Meggie," Lila warned Bella.

"As if I would," said Bella, grinning wickedly.

Lila watched the pair flutter up the Owl staircase, before walking toward the library door. She stroked her little unicorn charm for courage.

"Wish me luck," she told it. Then with a deep breath she lifted the latch on the heavy oak door and went in. Bee Balm was waiting in front of Mistress Hawthorn's desk. The librarian looked up at the sound of Lila's footsteps.

"Ah, there you are, Lilac Blossom," she said.

Lila stood next to Bee Balm and dropped Mistress Hawthorn a polite curtsy. On the far side of the library, half hidden by a bookshelf, Lila saw Sea Holly and Candytuft engrossed in a large black book.

"Wands, please," said Mistress Hawthorn, holding out her hand for them. She laid them side-by-side on her desk, out of reach, then passed each of the fairies a scroll. "Mistress Pipit wishes you to write out the line, 'Cooperation is better than disagreement: from cooperation friendship flows'. Do you understand what that means, Lilac Blossom?"

"Yes, I think so," Lila nodded. "It's better to help each other and not argue, because if fairies help each other they might become friends." She could almost imagine Bee Balm's furious glare burning her skin.

"Yes," said Mistress Hawthorn. "Perhaps writing that five hundred times might create a little cooperation between the two of you?"

Lila knew there was no chance of that, as she and Bee Balm sat down by the librarian's desk. She picked up the waiting quill, dipped it in the

# Frog Shock

ink and began to write her first line carefully in her best handwriting.

After what seemed ages, Lila looked up. She had been numbering each line so she would know how far she had gotten: two hundred and already she had a stiff wrist and aching fingers. She glanced across at Bee Balm, who hadn't completed nearly as many lines.

Another dip in the ink and Lila started on line two hundred and one. She was adding the period when a scream from the other side of the library made her jump and her quill left several inky blots.

"It's a spider. It's on my frock. Get it off. Get it off," the voice screeched.

Mistress Hawthorn got up and hurried across the library to find out what was happening. There was a huge crash of falling books, and, without thinking, Lila also ran to help. Candytuft was standing on the table weeping among the pile of scattered volumes. Lila picked up two that had fallen to the floor.

"Go back to your lines, at once," said the librarian finally noticing her. Lila returned to Mistress Hawthorn's desk to find Bee Balm busily writing as if there had been no disturbance at all.

"I'm terrified of spiders," Candytuft choked. "Especially black and hairy ones."

"I know you are," said Sea Holly, patting her sympathetically. She sent a glance in Bee Balm's direction and, with what Lila was certain was a wink, led the sobbing fairy from the library and calm was restored. Lila was instantly suspicious. What did that wink mean? But there was nothing she could do except continue writing.

With a great deal of tut-tutting Mistress Hawthorn took her seat again and for a while all was silence. By the time Lila had reached the end of line two hundred and seventy her hand was aching even more. But she kept going,

# Frog Shock

"Cooperation is better than disagreement: from cooperation friendship flows." It was so boring.

"Mistress Hawthorn, I've finished," said Bee Balm, putting down her quill and handing her scroll across the desk. The librarian took it and studied Bee Balm's work carefully.

*Impossible*, thought Lila. But Bee Balm was poised to go.

"Very well," said Mistress Hawthorn, handing back the Princess's wand. "Next time you come to the library, I hope it will be to look at the books." She dismissed the Princess with a nod and, bobbing quickly Bee Balm hurried away. "And have you nearly finished, Lilac Blossom?"

"Um, not quite," said Lila.

"Then onward, no slacking."

Lila hurried up as much as she dared while her thoughts raced. Now Sea Holly's wink made sense. She had deliberately frightened Candytuft with the spider to create a disturbance. It had been the perfect distraction, giving Bee Balm time to snatch up her wand and do a simple duplicating charm with the lines on the scroll. And time enough to put her wand back in place before anyone noticed what she had done. Typical, Bee Balm had gotten away with writing hardly any lines and here she was stuck with hundreds to go.

It seemed like she'd been writing forever, when Lila put in her last period at the end of line five hundred. She eased her fingers and waited while Mistress Hawthorn inspected the scroll.

"Neatly done, I must say," she told Lila.

Once she was dismissed, Lila hurried from the library as fast as she could, bumping into Candytuft, who was waiting outside.

"Are you all right now?" Lila asked kindly. "I'm sorry that spider frightened you."

"Thanks, I hate them," said the shy green fairy, without meeting Lila's eye. "Please, I was wondering if you would show me the transformation wand movement? You were really good at it this afternoon."

"Well, I'm not sure I was that good."

"Show me anyway," pleaded Candytuft, squeezing Lila's wrist until it hurt. "Please!"

"Ouch, Candytuft, that pinched."

"Sorry," said Candytuft, glancing anxiously over her shoulder. Lila showed Candytuft the movement twice.

"Can you show me one more time?" Candytuft begged. "I still haven't quite got it." Candytuft was tugging at her arm again and Lila was starting to feel cross with her.

"Bella, show Candytuft the transformation circle," called Lila, spotting her two friends hurrying toward her. "Just to make sure I've remembered it correctly." But when Lila turned around again Candytuft had gone.

"Something's happened," Bella said.

"My little web-woven bag's been stolen,"

# Stardust Surprise

Meggie whispered in Lila's ear.

"Stolen! Whoever would want to do a thing like that?" asked Lila.

"That's what I thought, at first," said Bella, with meaning. "But we've turned our room upside down and it's not there."

Lila remembered the incident in the Wishing Wood during their lesson.

"You don't think…?"

Bella nodded.

Thoughts whirled in Lila's head. Was it possible that Candytuft had stolen Meggie's bag? Could it have been the bag that she handed to Bee Balm in the wood? And did it explain Candytuft's odd behavior just now? The sooner they found out the answer to some of these questions the better.

## Chapter Six

# Suspicious Happenings

Back in their bedroom in the Star Clan turret Lila and Bella reminded Meggie of what they had seen in the Wishing Wood that afternoon.

"Whatever it was that Candytuft gave Bee Balm, it was tiny. We couldn't see it," Lila said. "It could easily have been your little bag."

"But Candytuft's in the Cloud Clan. Any fairies in the Star Clan common room would have asked her what she was doing in the Star turret. She couldn't have come in here," said Meggie.

# Stardust Surprise

"But we'd left the window open," said Bella. "She could have flown in."

"It's a possibility," said Lila. "We talked about your bag in class this morning. Everybody knew about it."

"But we can't accuse Candytuft," said Meggie. "Think how upset she'd be if we were wrong."

"No, of course, we can't," said Bella. "But it is an interesting coincidence, isn't it?"

"We can't prove anything though," said Meggie stubbornly. "It's just a guess."

"Meggie's right," said Lila. "And I'm guessing something else: I think Bee Balm cheated on her lines." She told her friends what had happened in the library.

"I'm certain Sea Holly deliberately frightened Candytuft with the spider. It gave Bee Balm plenty of time to do a quick duplicating charm while Mistress Hawthorn was away from her desk. I didn't finish my lines until ages later."

# Suspicious Happenings

"We wondered why Bee Balm had come out and you hadn't," said Meggie.

"Bella," said Lila, a thought popping into her head. "You didn't transform the bag into something else by accident did you?"

"No, I did not," said Bella. "Meggie and I made this for transformation practice!" She rummaged in her drawer and pulled out a rather good paper worm. "See, it even wiggles."

"Lila," said Meggie, sharply. "Where's your school bracelet?"

Lila looked down at her wrist. The silver chain that should have been hanging there was gone and with it her silver unicorn.

"I had it on before I went in the library," she said, numbly. "I asked my unicorn for good luck. Did I drop it when I came out, do you think?"

The three fairies hurriedly retraced their steps from the Star Clan turret, down the Owl staircase and back across the Hall of Rainbows.

# Stardust Surprise

The bracelet was nowhere to be seen. They stood by the library door.

"Mistress Hawthorn's really scary," said Lila, full of misgivings and not wanting to go inside.

"Let's report it to Pipity," said Meggie. "And maybe she'll ask Mistress Hawthorn to look for it."

"Okay," said Lila, feeling torn. She felt weak at the thought of having to go anywhere near Mistress Hawthorn again, even though she was desperate to find her bracelet and her silver unicorn. The three fairies trudged back up the Owl staircase to the refectory. Lila tiptoed to the teacher's table and gently tapped Mistress Pipit on the shoulder.

"What is it, Lilac Blossom?" Mistress Pipit asked, turning around.

"I've lost my school bracelet," Lila said in a half whisper, ashamed of being so careless, especially as Fairy Godmother Whimbrel was sitting next to

# Suspicious Happenings

Mistress Pipit and could hear everything she was saying. It was bad enough having to tell her teacher, let alone the Headteacher overhearing such a shameful confession.

"Have you looked for it?"

"Everywhere but in the library," said Lila.

"Two bracelets gone," exclaimed Mistress Pipit. "Whatever's going on? Well, if they haven't turned up by tomorrow we'll involve the whole school in a thorough search. In the meantime, perhaps you and Bee Balm could help each other look?"

Lila nodded and went back to the First Year's table.

"I saved you some dandelion fritters," said Bella, eagerly helping herself. "They'd nearly all gone."

"What did Pipity say?" Meggie asked.

"If the bracelets haven't turned up by tomorrow everyone will look. She also said Bee Balm and I should help each other search."

# Stardust Surprise

Bella almost choked on her mouthful. "Are you really going to offer to help Bee Balm?"

"I might," said Lila, but not with enthusiasm. "Thanks for getting me the fritters." Chewing slowly, Lila glanced across at the teacher's table. Mistress Pipit was talking intently to Fairy Godmother Whimbrel.

"Are you going to tell Pipity about your missing bag?" Lila asked Meggie, pushing her plate away.

"Tomorrow. It's not as important as losing a school bracelet and she won't want to hear about something else getting lost today."

"Stolen, you mean," said Bella, pulling Lila's discarded plate toward her. "Can I finish these?" And without waiting for an answer Bella helped herself to the remains of Lila's meal.

"I'm going back to the Star Clan turret," said Lila getting up.

"I'll catch up to you when I've finished," said Bella.

# Suspicious Happenings

"If you can move," laughed Meggie, getting up to go with Lila.

Bee Balm caught Lila's eye as she turned for the door. Candytuft glanced in her direction too. Bee Balm and Sea Holly exchanged a quick smile that gave Lila the uncomfortable feeling they were sharing a delicious secret. But they were ignoring Candytuft, who looked miserable and ready to leave the table. Lila grabbed Meggie's arm and hurried her outside.

"What?" said Meggie. Lila put a finger to her lips and waited. They stood there for a good minute before Candytuft came through the door.

"Hi, there," said Lila. "Are you over the shock of the spider yet?"

"Yes, what bad luck," added Meggie, with a shudder. "I hate spiders."

Candytuft stopped dead as though she had seen two ghosts.

"Oh hi," she said. "Y…yes, it was a shock!"

# Suspicious Happenings

"I don't suppose you've seen my school bracelet?" Lila asked. "I've lost it, you see." Candytuft shook her head slowly.

"Or my web-woven bag?" said Meggie. "It's disappeared from my bedroom."

"Don't ask me," said Candytuft, who had gone the palest of pale. "I don't know where they are." And she turned away and fluttered down the corridor as fast as her wings would fly her.

"What do you make of that?" asked Lila.

"Odd. Candytuft's usually so pleasant and friendly," Meggie replied. "I've never seen such a guilty-looking fairy."

"But guilty about what?" pondered Lila. "Stealing your bag or my bracelet or something else?" Meggie shrugged and the two of them strolled thoughtfully back to the Star Clan turret.

Bella didn't join them until ages later. When she finally burst into the bedroom she was jumping with excitement and hiccupping loudly.

# Stardust Surprise

"Guess what, hic, I've just seen? Hic!" she said.

"Oh honestly, Bella," said Meggie. "You've eaten too much. Drink from the wrong side of this." She handed Bella a glass of water. Bella drank and spluttered.

"Hic...I followed...Bee Balm and Sea Holly back to our classroom, hic, only they heard me coming, so I had to pretend...hic...I had forgotten my scroll."

"What were they doing?" Lila asked.

"That's the interesting thing," said Bella. "Hic... When I went in they'd opened the door to Pipity's cabinet but when they saw me they moved away and pretended to do something else. The problem was, once I'd gotten the scroll I had to go and I couldn't listen outside because of the...hic... hiccups."

"If you hadn't been so greedy you might have found out more," said Meggie. Bella shrugged and took another sip of water.

# Suspicious Happenings

"We must be on our guard tomorrow," Lila said, rubbing her empty wrist. "At least my wand didn't get broken this morning, thanks to you, Bella. At least I've still got that."

"Oh Lila," said Meggie. "We'll find your bracelet. Really we will."

"Yes, and if we don't," said Bella, "I'm sure Pipity can give you another one."

Meggie shot Bella a warning look.

"I don't mind a new school bracelet but I want my unicorn back," said Lila.

"Listen," said Bella. "The unicorn chose you, now that it's lost perhaps it'll find you. It is magic after all. Don't forget that." She gave another great hiccup.

"Thanks, Bella, you're right," smiled Lila. "If I can't find it, maybe it'll find me." And with that comforting thought she had to be content.

## Chapter Seven

# Nighttime Search

That night in bed Lila tossed and turned but could not get to sleep. The day's events kept playing over and over again in her head.

Lila's fingers searched for the comfort of her silver unicorn. Of course, it wasn't there. She sat up. If she hadn't turned Bee Balm into a frog, the Princess wouldn't have lost her bracelet. Once she'd thought it Lila couldn't get away from the idea. Mistress Pipit had told her that she and Bee Balm should help each other. Lila reached for her

# Nighttime Search

wand and, with a little shake, lit up its star. Meggie and Bella were fast asleep. Rather than lie awake thinking, she would look for Bee Balm's bracelet in the place where she was certain it must still be and when she found it she would look for her own.

Lila slipped from her bed and dressed quickly. Flicking out the wand light she fluttered to the window and pushed it open. There were stars in the sky and a waxing moon. But the garden was full of shadows and the trees of the Wishing Wood loomed dark and forbidding.

Undaunted, Lila held tight to her wand and fluttered from the windowsill, down, down into the shadows. She landed lightly on the grass. The garden was silent apart from the pattering water falling from the mermaid fountain. The four clan turrets loomed high into the night sky and through the tall arched windows of the Hall of Rainbows the great chandeliers were dimly flickering.

# Stardust Surprise

She turned toward the gatehouse where Captain Klop the fierce old sea dragon lived. As guardian of the gate, he patrolled the grounds at night and she didn't want him to catch her. He was famous for his bad temper.

Keeping alert Lila tiptoed across the grass toward the Bewitching Pool. She dipped a toe in the chilly water, flicked alight the star on her wand and, with a deep breath, dived in.

The fish swished golden tails in protest at Lila's sudden intrusion into the green water. She was sorry to have startled them but she didn't have much time to search. The blood was already pounding in her head and she was soon forced to the surface to breathe. It was going to take ages to search the whole pool, unless…she quickly made up her mind.

"I'll dream wish myself into a fairy fish," she told herself. "That way I can stay under water for as long as I like."

# Nighttime Search

Lila closed her eyes and concentrated, imagining her wings smaller, until they were gills on her back, perfect for breathing under water. She stretched her arm over her shoulder and touched her wings with her wand.

Her back prickled and she found breathing through her mouth made her gasp. The dream wish had worked. She quickly dived between the lily stems and the weeds and began her search in earnest. The gills worked beautifully underwater. The fish and the frogs clustered around her curiously. Holding her wand tightly to light the way, she explored from one end of the pool to the other, but she could not find the bracelet anywhere.

She was about to give up when a golden carp swam ahead of her then turned and waited. Lila swam cautiously toward it. The fish moved further away then waited again. This time, when Lila caught up with the carp, it dived steeply and

# Stardust Surprise

Lila did the same. Down they went, deeper and deeper, to the bottom of the pool. The fish settled itself on the mud and swished its tail. A great cloud of silt rose up and through the clearing water Lila saw a glint of silver. She dived forward and her hand closed around a chain bracelet.

*It was buried*, thought Lila. *That was why Pipity couldn't find it.* She shot to the surface as the dream wish faded and her wings returned. "Thank you, beautiful fish, for helping me," she called gently across the water.

Back on the bank she took several deep breaths of fresh night air. A silver fox charm glinted in the moonlight. It was definitely Bee Balm's bracelet.

She pocketed it and, after squeezing out her frock as best she could, ran across the grass to the great door of the Hall of Rainbows.

The latch, which usually opened smoothly and easily, wouldn't budge. *No school bracelet, no entry into the Hall of Rainbows,* Lila reminded herself.

# Stardust Surprise

She pulled out Bee Balm's silver chain. It was time to use it. She had to put down her wand and struggle really hard to get it on her wrist. It made her feel strangely limp and she had almost no strength to lift the latch. Somehow she managed it and the door finally swung open. She took the bracelet off the moment she was in the Hall of Rainbows and put it back in her pocket.

"Whew," she whispered. "I'm not putting that on again in a hurry. It didn't like me wearing it one bit."

Keeping to the wall, Lila went silently toward the library. The dim light from the chandeliers gave just enough light. Finding Bee Balm's bracelet had cheered her up. She was certain hers had to be somewhere on the floor by Mistress Hawthorn's table. She slipped silently inside the library, closing the door behind her.

It was much darker in here than in the Hall of Rainbows. It took a few moments for her eyes to

# Nighttime Search

make out the shadow of Mistress Hawthorn's table. Lila tiptoed toward it. She was about to light up her wand when she heard a clump as though someone had put down a heavy book. The sound came from the far side of the room. Lila dropped to the floor and, with a pounding heart, slipped underneath the table. Someone else was in the library.

## Chapter Eight

# Terror and Truce

Cautiously, Lila felt around the floor for her bracelet. She had felt certain it would be there but she couldn't find it. It was a horrible disappointment. As she wondered what to do next she heard another bump.

"Oh, this is so fiddly!" someone said crossly.

To Lila's surprise the voice sounded like Bee Balm's. Curiosity gave her the courage to come out from under the table and creep to the nearest bookshelf. If it was the Princess, what was she doing in the library in the middle of the night? There was the shuffle of turning pages and an irritable grunt. From her hiding place, Lila took a quick peek. The far corner of the library was lit up by the glow of wand light. She could just make out Bee Balm reading from a large black and gold book. But what else was she doing? It looked like she had fit the handle of her wand inside a web-woven bag. Whatever for?

Lila stepped quietly from behind the bookshelf and moved forward, her wand at the ready in case Bee Balm turned around. Now she could see that the Princess was struggling to stick the web-woven bag to the wand's handle.

"Done it at last. Let's see if it works," said Bee Balm to herself, gripping the wand firmly. The sun at its tip glowed with a fierce and bright light.

"Power," said the Princess. "How fantastic is that! Now all I've got to do is make the bag invisible so nobody can see it on the handle. That should be easy enough. And then I will have a truly magnificent wand."

Lila gave a little cough and the Princess spun around with a horrified gasp.

"You! What are you doing here?"

"I'm looking for my bracelet," said Lila. "What are you doing here?"

"A bit of research," said Bee Balm, quickly closing the book to hide the page she'd been looking at.

"With Meggie's web-woven bag!"

"This is *my* bag. *I* don't steal things."

"No, you get other fairies to do your stealing for you. See those yellow-ocher stitches? That's Meggie's special mark. It means it's Meggie's bag."

Bee Balm quickly gathered her thoughts.

"I asked Candytuft to find me a web-woven bag. I don't know where she got it from," she said, eventually.

Lila let the lie pass. Instead she said, "Mistress

# Terror and Truce

Pipit suggested I should help you look for your school bracelet. Would you like to help me look for mine?"

"No, I would not," said Bee Balm. "Who do you think I am? I wouldn't dream of looking for your silly bracelet."

"Very well, I'll put yours back where I found it," said Lila with a shrug.

"What do you mean?" Bee Balm said. "You're trying to make a fool of me, aren't you? I don't believe you've got my bracelet. You're bluffing."

"I had a real struggle using it to get into the Hall of Rainbows from the garden," said Lila. "It didn't like me wearing it one bit."

Bee Balm gave Lila a long hard stare, but both fairies turned quickly as the library door creaked open and three things happened very fast. Bee Balm shook out her wand light. Lila grabbed the Princess's arm and dragged her into the fireplace and a sudden bright light lit up the whole library.

# Stardust Surprise

"Is somebody in here? Come out at once!"

The voice was chilling. Both the Princess and Lila were wedged firmly in the chimney and neither of them had any intention of giving themselves up to Mistress Hawthorn.

"Oh, look at that," said the librarian crossly, reaching the table where Bee Balm had been sitting. "A book left out. How careless," she muttered. "It will not do!" She put the book back in its place on the shelf and continued her inspection.

Both Lila and Bee Balm breathed a sigh of relief when Mistress Hawthorn finally left and closed the door behind her. But then they heard the sound of a key turning: they had been locked in.

"There's nothing else to do," said Bee Balm. "I'm getting out of here and I suppose I'm going to have to take you with me if I want my bracelet back!"

"No, thank you," said Lila.

# Terror and Truce

"You don't have a choice," said Bee Balm and she grabbed hold of Lila's wand.

"Power up!" she cried, her own wand exploding like a rocket. The two fairies shot up the chimney at terrifying speed and out into the night sky. Up they went higher and higher, higher than Lila had ever been before, almost up to the stars.

"What have you been doing?" Lila cried, when she felt able to talk again. "This isn't right!"

"Mind your own business," cried Bee Balm, letting go of Lila's wand at last.

Looking down Lila saw how small Silverlake Fairy School had become while the waters of the Great Silver Lake spread wide below them. *This is what it must be like to collect stardust when the moon is full*, she thought. *Lucky Fifth Years!* But she also knew she must get back and swooped earthward. Bee Balm followed her.

Lila tried in vain to fly inside the castle walls. She was pushed away by the protecting charms, as

she knew she would be, and ended up landing on the jetty. The drawbridge was up but she didn't dare shout for Captain Klop.

"What have you done to your wand?" Lila asked, when Bee Balm landed beside her.

"Nothing that has anything to do with you," said the Princess. "Besides, you should be pleased it got you out of the library. There's not enough power in your purple stick to do that. Now hand over my bracelet."

"And trust you to get me back into school?" said Lila. "I don't think so."

"You're not in any position to make conditions, Pots-and-Pans. Hand it over."

A familiar tingling ran up Lila's spine. It was telling her something. All she had to do was... what did she have to do? Yes, she had to dream wish her unicorn charm. Call her unicorn to her. It felt very close by. Why hadn't she thought of doing that before?

# Stardust Surprise

She moved away from Bee Balm to give herself plenty of space and closed her eyes. She held out her wand and spun around slowly. In her mind she could see the unicorn, surrounded by silver stars. "Gallop to me, little unicorn," she whispered. "Gallop to me!"

"Stop it, Lilac Blossom," said Bee Balm. "What are you doing?"

Lila opened her eyes to find her wand pointing directly at Bee Balm. In the Princess's outstretched hand was a silver bracelet and attached was a tiny silver unicorn charm. It looked as though it was galloping through the air, dragging the Princess along behind.

"Let go," cried Lila.

"Never," shouted Bee Balm.

Lila quickly reached into her pocket.

"Your bracelet for mine," she said, eyes ablaze. "A fox for a unicorn." And she tossed Bee Balm's bracelet into the air. It turned over and over and over. With a screech, Bee Balm let go of Lila's unicorn and flew from the jetty to save her silver fox. At last Lila had the little unicorn charm back on her wrist.

Bee Balm fluttered to the jetty in a rage.

"You stupid fairy," she said to Lila. "I barely caught my fox. He nearly went in the lake."

"I've already dived for him once. I would have gone again. Besides, you have some explaining to do. Come on." Lila took off, flying up over the castle wall. Her bracelet gave a comforting tingle as she flew into the school grounds. She landed in the garden with Bee Balm dropping down beside her.

"I don't have to explain anything to you," the Princess snapped.

But before Lila could reply, Bella and Meggie fluttered across from the shadows.

"I think you do," Bella said. "Candytuft woke us because she was feeling so guilty. She's told us everything."

# Stardust Surprise

"Yes, and we must make things right at once, before any of the teachers find out what you've done," Meggie added.

Five minutes later all four fairies arrived in the Charm One classroom.

"I don't see why I have to do what you tell me to," said Bee Balm, defiantly.

"Oh, but you do," said Bella. "Don't you realize how lucky you are that Pipity hasn't found out what you've been up to? You could be expelled."

"I only borrowed it," huffed Bee Balm.

"Four grains of stardust?" said Bella. "Pipity showed us how powerful one grain was and you took *four* from her bag in the cabinet!"

"You used poor Candytuft to steal my web-woven bag to put it in and you persuaded her to take Lila's unicorn bracelet," said Meggie.

"So, that explains why Candytuft kept grabbing my arm so strangely outside the library," gasped Lila. "No one's going to get away with stealing my bracelet like that a second time."

"It was to pay you back for turning me into a frog, you dishcloth you," said Bee Balm. "It was all your fault I lost my bracelet."

"It was a genuine accident," said Bella. "And you know it."

"Anyway, I wanted a more powerful wand. What's wrong with that?" said Bee Balm.

"Everything, if you have to lie and cheat to get it," said Lila. "Now, if you put the stardust back and give Meggie her bag, we'll agree to say nothing."

"Big deal," huffed the Princess.

"Just because you're a princess doesn't mean you can't be expelled," said Bella.

"They wouldn't dare!"

"If you believe that, you don't know Fairy Godmother Whimbrel," said Bella.

Bee Balm opened her mouth to say something else but thought better of it. Instead she slid the web-woven bag from her wand's handle.

# Stardust Surprise

"All right, you win," she grumbled. "I'll put the stardust back." Lila took out Mistress Pipit's web-woven bag from the cabinet. The stardust inside glittered brightly when she opened it and the three fairies watched carefully as the four grains of stardust were shaken back where they belonged. Then Lila quickly pulled the drawstring tight and returned the bag to the cabinet. Bee Balm tossed Meggie her bag.

"Truce?" Lila asked. "You keep away from us and we'll keep away from you."

"I suppose, if you promise to say nothing."

"If you keep to the truce," said Lila, "we promise not to say a word."

"Agreed," said Bee Balm, and, with a flounce, she left the classroom.

"I don't believe it!" said Bella with an astonished smile.

"Peace at last," said Lila. "What a relief!"

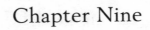

Chapter Nine

# The Wand Skills Charm Examination

The next morning some very tired fairies were finding it difficult to stay awake in class.

"Let's hope Pipity thinks it's because we've been working for the Wand Skills Charm Examination," yawned Lila. From now until the exam, lessons were to be given to review and, by the end of the afternoon, Lila thought the day had gone well.

"Bee Balm hasn't argued with us, or been mean in any way," said Lila. "She's even spoken kindly to Candytuft."

"I know," sighed Meggie. "I just hope Candytuft never behaves that badly again just to keep in with her. I don't exactly trust Bee Balm, but for now she does seem to be doing the right thing."

"Now what we have to do is earn some clan points to make up for the ones we lost in the library," said Lila. "That would please Musk Mallow."

"And pass the test," said Bella. "I'm going to get the paper worm. We can practice transformation in the garden."

Lila sat next to Meggie by the Bewitching Pool to enjoy the sunlight while they waited. "If Bee Balm was like this all the time, it would be bliss," she sighed.

"Enjoy it while it lasts," said Meggie. "She takes being a haughty princess very seriously. She'll never be able to keep up this behavior."

# The Wand Skills Charm Examination

Lila spread out her wings and lay on her back chuckling.

"You may be right, Meggie." But for now Lila didn't care. She had her bracelet back and so did Bee Balm. All was well. She touched her little unicorn with her wand. "Silver Toes, Golden Boy, White Wisp, Firecracker," she chanted.

"What lovely names," said Meggie.

"But the wrong ones," said Lila. "How am I ever going to find the right one?"

"When the time's right, you will," said Meggie. "It'll happen just like that."

"I hope so," said Lila. "But I'll never lose him again. Not now I can dream wish him back to me."

Meggie tapped Lila's arm. Bee Balm and Sea Holly had settled themselves on the far side of the pool.

"We'll keep our distance," said Lila. "For safety's sake."

"Ready?" Bella asked, arriving with the paper

worm. "Me first. I'm going to do a silly one," she said, dropping the worm then twirling and pointing her wand. "Jumping inkwell."

There was a puff of sky-blue stars and an inkwell shot into the air spraying black ink everywhere.

"Watch out," cried Lila, leaping out of the way while Bella collapsed in a fit of the giggles.

The inkwell leaped higher and higher until it took off across the Bewitching Pool heading straight for Bee Balm. Lila dashed after it, pointing her wand and shouting, "Teddy bear."

A cuddly toy landed beside the Princess.

"That was a near miss, Pots-and-Pans," Bee Balm said. "Was that inkwell another accident?"

"Yes, sorry," said Lila, grabbing the toy. "It really was." Lila beckoned Bella and Meggie indoors.

"I didn't think it would leap the Bewitching Pool," said Bella, apologetically.

# Stardust Surprise

"What if it had covered Bee Balm with ink?" said Meggie. "It's lucky Lila managed to transform it in time."

"Yes, from now on we must be very, very careful," said Lila. Bella bit her lip and nodded. They took the bear back to the Star Clan turret and practiced in their room, where it was safer.

The morning of the Wand Skills Charm Examination soon arrived and a class of nervous fairies sat at their mushroom desks with blank scrolls in front of them.

"There's no need to look so scared," said Mistress Pipit, with a smile. "You have all worked very hard for this exam and I'm sure that you'll all do very well on the written paper. As you know, you'll take the practical test after break."

Lila and Meggie smiled encouragingly at Bella. They knew how hard she had studied and practiced. Lila had never seen Bella nervous before and, most unusually, she had only eaten one bowl of heather honey porridge for breakfast. Bee Balm sat confidently at the front, regally arranging her pink gossamer frock before picking up her quill ready to start.

"Very well," said Mistress Pipit. "You may begin now."

Six questions appeared on the board. Lila quickly read them. None was difficult. They had covered everything in their review. And Bella had learned all she needed to answer the questions. Lila glanced around. Bella was already writing. With a pleased smile, Lila began to do the same.

It seemed as though no time at all had passed when Mistress Pipit said, "Finish your sentence and put down your quills."

Bella looked up, flushed, but with a grin. Meggie too was smiling. With a flick of her wand,

# Stardust Surprise

Mistress Pipit gathered in the scrolls, which flocked together and made a neat pile on her table.

"Now, we are going to do our practical Wand Skills Examination in the Hall of Rainbows. Fairy Godmother Whimbrel will be there to watch." There were a few worried voices. "Let me remind you not to get too nervous," said Mistress Pipit. "Just do your best."

The bells rang for break and Bee Balm and Sea Holly were first out of the classroom. Lila, Meggie and Bella huddled together to go over the test.

"I've done better than I ever have before," said Bella. "It makes such a difference when you actually know stuff."

"Yes," Lila laughed. "It does. I was so glad to see you writing all through the exam."

"I could have gone on and on," said Bella. "It was great."

"You see, all that hard work was worth it," smiled Meggie.

# The Wand Skills Charm Examination

After break the class gathered in the Hall of Rainbows. Mistress Pipit and Fairy Godmother Whimbrel arrived together. Mistress Pipit made sure the Headteacher was comfortable on her silver throne. She sat with a scroll in her lap and a quill in her hand. It looked as though she was going to help Mistress Pipit with the marking.

"Do your best, fairies," she said, looking down at the class over her spectacles. "And enjoy yourselves."

After their nerves wore off the practical exam was lots of fun. The class stood in a circle with a paper worm in the center and each took a turn. The first time around Mistress Pipit told them what to charm. That was easy enough. The second time they could choose an object to transform, like a button or a pen, and all went smoothly.

"This time choose whatever you like, but be sensible," said Mistress Pipit on their third try. "Remember you are not to leave the circle."

# Stardust Surprise

Lila, whose turn came after Bella's, said, "Please, don't do a jumping anything."

"I won't," Bella grinned. But when her turn came, after Candytuft's, Bella gave an excited twirl of her wand, and turned Candytuft's hedgehog into a flying umbrella. It went as high as the ceiling in one flap. Luckily, Lila's aim was exact and she turned the umbrella into a flying squirrel, not exactly what she had intended to do, but at least it worked. Meggie sensibly waited for the squirrel to drop back into the circle before turning it into a tabby kitten.

"Honestly, Bella," whispered Lila.

"You're good at this," said Bella. "I just wanted them to see *how* good."

Bee Balm played safe with a butterfly that managed a little flutter and Sea Holly made a bluebird. Everyone did well and nobody made a mistake.

"Fairy Godmother Whimbrel and I will

announce the Wand Skills Charm Examination results this afternoon," Mistress Pipit said. "Well done, everyone."

"Showing off were we, Harebell?" said Bee Balm as they made their way to the refectory at lunchtime. Then she changed her tone. "Actually, I thought the flying umbrella was rather good."

"Oh, thanks, Bee Balm," said Bella, fumbling for something nice to say back. "Your butterfly was…very good too!"

"Yes, I try to please," said the Princess. "It was a particularly rare variety."

"Were we supposed to know that?" Bella whispered.

Lila and Meggie clasped their hands over their mouths in an effort not to laugh.

"Trust Bee Balm to go one better than everyone else," whispered Meggie.

"But she is trying," said Lila.

"Very trying," said Bella.

# Stardust Surprise

When it was time for the results, Fairy Godmother Whimbrel joined Mistress Pipit in the Charm One classroom.

"What promising First Year pupils we have. I'm proud of you all," beamed the Headteacher. "And I'm delighted to tell you that you've all passed. Each of you will receive your Wand Skills charm at the winter assembly. So that is something to look forward to – a second charm to add to your Silverlake Fairy School bracelets."

Bella jumped up, bursting with joy.

"I've passed!" she told Lila. "I've passed," she grinned at Meggie.

"The individual marks are on the board for you to look at," smiled Mistress Pipit, kindly ignoring Bella's unruly display. "I'll give back your exam scrolls in the morning. Well done all of you. A clan point each."

Bella hurried to find out her marks.

"Look, I've beaten Bee Balm by five," said

# The Wand Skills Charm Examination

Bella. "Lila, you're top. It must have been that fantastic transformation charm you did. And Meggie, you're second. That's fantastic!"

"Not such a mud-brain after all," Lila whispered into Bella's ear as Bee Balm stared at her friend with an expression of disbelief, clearly shocked that Bella had higher marks than she did.

After the excitement had died down and the bells had rung for the end of lessons Mistress Pipit asked Lila and Bee Balm to stay behind.

"I'm glad to see that you two have stopped squabbling," she said. "I'd like to think that writing out, 'Cooperation is better than disagreement: from cooperation friendship flows', five hundred times might have played some part in this peaceful outcome. And I'd like to reward you both with two extra clan points each for effort."

Lila blushed, knowing how far her teacher was from understanding the real reason for the present calm, but Bee Balm had no scruples.

# Stardust Surprise

"The lines really made me think, Mistress Pipit," she said. "I was grateful that I had to write them so many times."

"I'm glad to hear it," said Mistress Pipit.

Lila glanced at the Princess. How could she tell such a brazen lie? She was impossible. *Sooner or later*, Lila thought, *when it suits her, Bee Balm will forget the truce and something else will happen.*

But still, Lila had come top in the Wand Skills Charm Examination, made up the lost clan points and, for the moment, though she wasn't a friend of the Princess's, she was no longer an enemy. Tonight Lila would write a letter home to Cook and what a tale she had to tell her!

For a taste of Lila's next
fairy school adventure, read...

Silverlake
Fairy School
Bugs *and*
Butterflies

"Good morning, fairies," the Headteacher
said.

"Good morning, Fairy Godmother Whimbrel,"
the pupils replied, curtsying then making
themselves comfortable again.

"Now the first thing we're going to do at this
morning's assembly is the ribbon draw. I know
you're very excited about the first Bugs and
Butterflies matches of the season. In a few minutes
I will reveal which clan is playing against which."

Bella grinned.

*So that was what the assembly was about.* Lila grinned back, her tummy fluttering with excitement. *What was going to happen next?*

"Last year's winners were the Sun Clan..." Cheers broke out from the Sun Clan fairies and Fairy Godmother Whimbrel good-naturedly raised her wand for silence. "And the trophy will remain on display here in the Hall of Rainbows, decorated with its orange ribbon, until this year's champions are decided in the summer."

Lila closed her eyes and imagined the trophy with a silver Star Clan ribbon instead of an orange Sun Clan one. If only, if only!

"And now for the first draw of the year," Fairy Godmother Whimbrel said. With a wave of her wand a flurry of silver, white, yellow and orange ribbons danced above her head: silver for the Star Clan, orange for the Sun Clan, white for the Cloud Clan and yellow for the Moon Clan. With another commanding wave the ribbons paired, tying themselves into two bows, one a mix of silver and orange ribbon, the other a mix of white and yellow.

"The draw is made," smiled Fairy Godmother Whimbrel as the bows shimmered in the air. "The Moons will play the Clouds and the Stars will play the Suns. I wish all the players the very best of luck." There were cheers and a round of applause. Lila couldn't help a glance in Bee Balm's direction. The Princess was cheering as loudly as anyone. Lila smiled ruefully, for now the draw had made them real rivals.

To find out what
happens next, read

Silverlake
Fairy School
Bugs and
Butterflies

Join Lila and her friends
for more magical adventures at

www.silverlakefairyschool.com

# Unicorn Dreams

Lila longs to go to Silverlake Fairy School to learn about wands, charms and fairy magic – but spoiled Princess Bee Balm is set on ruining Lila's chances! Luckily nothing can stop Lila from following her dreams...

# Wands and Charms

It's Lila's first day at Silverlake Fairy School, and she's delighted to receive her first fairy charm and her own wand. But Lila quickly ends up breaking the school rules when bossy Princess Bee Balm gets her into trouble. Could Lila's school days be numbered...?

# Ready to Fly

Lila and her friends love learning to fly at Silverlake Fairy School. Their lessons in the Flutter Tower are a little scary but fantastic fun. Then someone plays a trick on Lila and she's grounded. Only Princess Bee Balm would be so mean. But how can Lila prove it?

# Bugs and Butterflies

Bugs and Butterflies is the magical game played at Silverlake Fairy School. Lila dreams of being picked to play for her clan's team, and she has a good chance, too, until someone starts cheating! Princess Bee Balm is also being unusually friendly to Lila...so what's going on?

# Dancing Magic

It's the beginning of winter at Silverlake Fairy School, and Lila and her friends are practicing to put on a spectacular show. There's a wonderful surprise in store for Lila too – one she didn't dare dream was possible!

# About the Author

Elizabeth Lindsay trained as a drama teacher before becoming a puppeteer on children's television. Elizabeth has published over thirty books, as well as writing numerous radio and television scripts including episodes of *The Hoobs*. Elizabeth dreams up adventures for Lilac Blossom from her attic in Gloucestershire, where she enjoys fairytale views down to the River Severn valley. If Elizabeth could go to Silverlake Fairy School, she would like a silver wand with a star at its tip, as she'd hope to be with Lila in the Star Clan. Like Lila, Elizabeth's favorite color is purple.